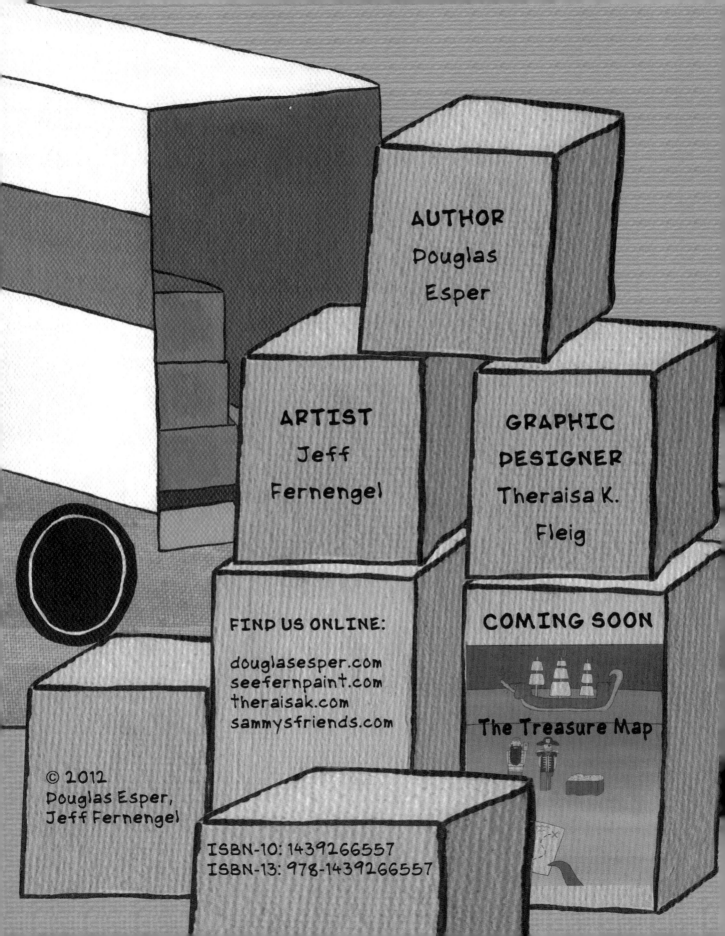

AUTHOR
Douglas Esper

ARTIST
Jeff Fernengel

GRAPHIC DESIGNER
Theraisa K. Fleig

FIND US ONLINE:

douglasesper.com
seefernpaint.com
theraisak.com
sammysfriends.com

COMING SOON

The Treasure Map

ISBN-10: 1439266557
ISBN-13: 978-1439266557

Jeff would like to dedicate this book to: Reese Fernengel; Theraisa to her kids: Haydin and Abigale Thompson; and Douglas to: Mara Rose and to all the friends who made me feel welcome each time I was the new kid in town. We would also like to thank Greg Fernengel

"Good morning Stephanie," Sammy said as he grabbed his fork.

"Sammy, before you eat you need to do your morning chore," Sammy's mother told him while she finished cooking.

Each morning Sammy counted the ripe tomatoes in his garden for his mother.

"I'll go right away!" Sammy said as he went to the door.

Sammy counted the
tomatoes.

How many tomatoes
do you count?

"Mother, there are fifteen ripe tomatoes!"

"Great counting Sammy. Tonight I will need four tomatoes for dinner.

When you get home from baseball practice will you grab them for me?" Sammy's mother asked.

"Sure thing," he responded.

Sammy looked at the house across the street and noticed that the new neighbors were moving in!

He saw a Mom and a Dad.

Their son was hidden behind boxes, so Sammy could not see him.

He waved, but the boy did not wave back.

"Mom, I waved at the new neighbors' son, but he did not wave back," Sammy said, confused.

"He is probably nervous to be in a new town," Sammy's mother replied.

Sammy quickly ate his breakfast and then raced off to his first baseball practice.

This year his team would be led by Bobby, the best pitcher in town.

Just as Sammy was passing his favorite pond, something struck him on the shoulder.

It did not hurt, but it surprised him.

Sammy saw someone move behind a tree but couldn't see who it was. He ran the rest of the way to practice.

"Sammy!" shouted various members of the team when they saw him arrive at the field.

The team was already starting to stretch. Sammy got in line with his friends.

He told them, "Someone threw a tomato at me, but I am not hurt."

That's when Sammy saw his good friend Bobby in a wheelchair!

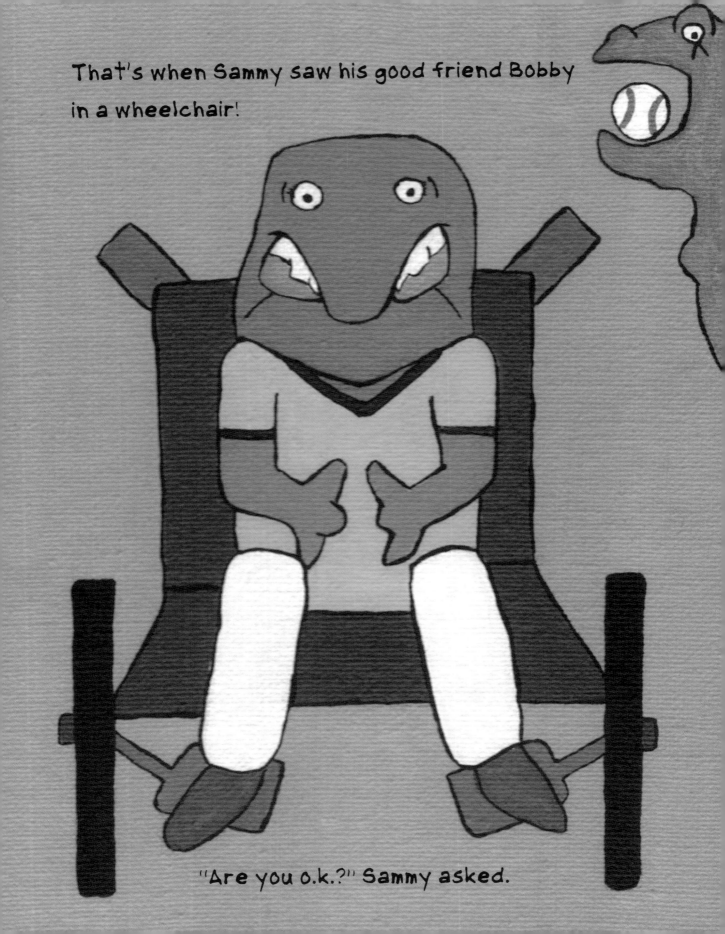

"Are you o.k.?" Sammy asked.

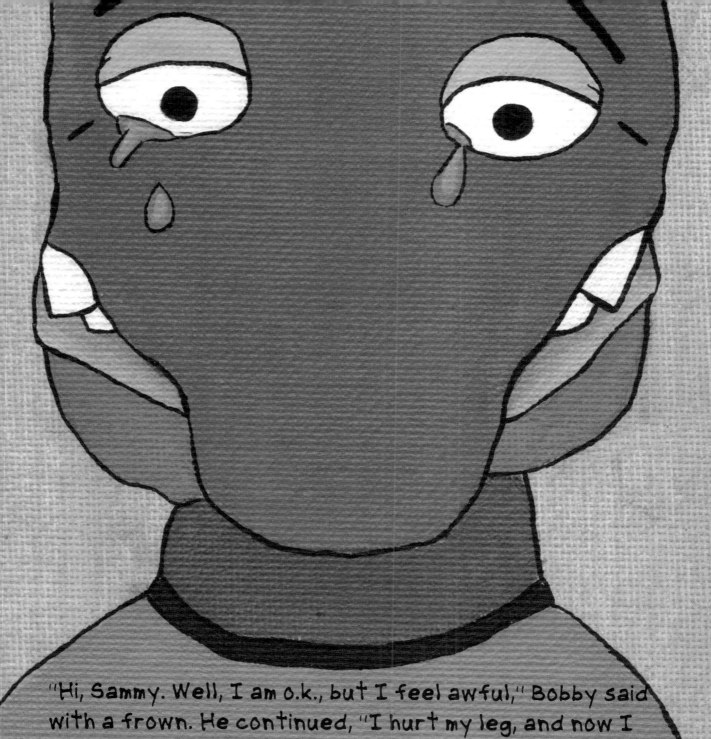

"Hi, Sammy. Well, I am o.k., but I feel awful," Bobby said
with a frown. He continued, "I hurt my leg, and now I
can't pitch. I really let the team down. I think I am
going to go home."

Bobby turned his wheelchair around and began to
head home.

"Bobby, don't go! You are a part of this team." said Sammy.

Bobby looked back at his teammates and asked, "Really, can I really stay?"

"Of course we want you to stay, Bobby!" said Jeff.

"We are your friends, no matter what," added Susan.

After practice, Sammy walked home with Jeff and Susan. Sammy boasted that he had fifteen ripe tomatoes in his garden.

Just then, Jeff was hit with a tomato!

Although Jeff told his friends that he was fine, his feelings were hurt when he heard the mysterious thrower laughing.

They got to Sammy's house, and he proudly displayed his tomatoes to his friends.

"They look great Sammy," said Susan.

"Yes, they do," added Jeff, "but there are only thirteen tomatoes now."

Sammy counted:

The next morning Sammy left for school with a tomato for show and tell. He was glad when he counted eight tomatoes still on his plant. There were no more missing tomatoes.

"Good morning," Sammy said, happy to see his friends.

They started walking up the hill to school when
Susan was hit with a tomato this time. All three
friends could hear the person laughing. He was hiding
behind a tree.

"Ouch!" Susan said
as she rubbed
her shoulder.

Susan runs fast,
but even she
couldn't catch
the tomato
thrower.

At school, Mrs. Hooks told the class, "Today we welcome a new student. His name is Tom. He just moved to Fern Valley."

At recess, Susan was going to race John, one of the older boys, when Bobby yelled out and surprised her.

Susan looked and saw that the tomato thrower had struck again!

"Wow!" Bobby said as he pointed to a shadow hiding behind a tree.

"Do you know who that is?" asked Sammy.

"No," he replied, "but I do know they have a great throwing arm. Look how far away they are!"

Susan said, "Yes, it was a terrific throw."

"I have an idea," said Sammy, "Tonight let's hide by my tomato plant. I think we will find out who our mysterious tomato thrower is."

Bobby, Jeff, Susan, and
Sammy waited and waited
by the garden.

They counted the
tomatoes again.

How many tomatoes are left?

They counted together:

As the Fern Valley friends
hid behind a tree, they
heard a noise.

They looked and saw someone
picking another tomato!

"Tom, why are you throwing tomatoes at us?" asked Sammy.

"You don't like me because I am different," said Tom. Then he asked, "So are you going to tell on me now?"

"Yes!" said Bobby, Susan, and Jeff all at once.

Tom started to cry.

"No," said Sammy.

Sammy's friends looked at him, surprised.

"Are you going to hit me?" Tom asked as he cried.

"No," said Sammy, "I am going to ask you to be on our baseball team."

Tom stopped crying. Now all the kids looked at Sammy, even more surprised.

"What?" they all asked.

"With Bobby hurt, the team needs a pitcher this year. With your arm, I think you would be a great pitcher." Sammy explained.

"You would want me to pitch on your team?" Tom asked as he wiped away tears.

They all responded:

They all laughed
together as friends.
Tom was so happy he
moved to Fern Valley.
Sammy was happy too.

21634391R00028

Made in the USA
Lexington, KY
21 March 2013